P IS FOR POPPADOMS!

An Indian Alphabet Book

by Kabir Sehgal & Surishtha Sehgal

illustrated by Hazel Ito

Beach Lane Books • New York   London   Toronto   Sydney   New Delhi

A is for Aam.

The **aam**, mango, is the national fruit of India, and India produces about half of all the mangoes in the world. There are many types of mangoes, including the Alphonso, which is sweet and juicy.

B is for Bandar.

Bandars, monkeys, roam through many parts of India. They sometimes take people's food, cameras, and even books!

C is for Chai.

Chai, Indian tea, has spices like cinnamon, cardamom, ginger, and cloves. It also comes with sugar and plenty of milk. India produces the second largest amount of tea in the world, after China. Darjeeling and Assam are regions in India that have become famous for their teas.

D is for Diwali.

Diwali, the Festival of Light, is India's grandest festival, which occurs in fall. It represents the victory of good over evil and light over darkness. People light candles throughout their houses and ignite fireworks in the streets.

E is for Ek.

Can you count to three in Hindi? **Ek** (one, एक), **do** (two, दो), **teen** (three, तीन). Indians invented the number **shoony** (zero, शून्य) in the seventh century.

F is for Falooda.

Falooda is a cold dessert that is made of vermicelli or thin noodles. Other ingredients include rose syrup, basil seeds, milk, and ice cream.

G is for Guru.

A **guru** is a spiritual guide or a teacher who has mastered a field of knowledge. A guru shares wisdom things like what books to read, how to exercise, or how to live in a peaceful manner.

H is for Haathee.

Haathees, elephants, live in forests and national parks across India and are occasionally seen walking down the street with a human keeper. Haathees have large brains and are wise and strong.

I is for Imalee.

TAMARIND CHUTNEY

Delicious
with
Poppadoms, Meat, Fish!

Imalee, tamarind, is a fruit that tastes both sweet and sour, and it is used to flavor many dishes. India is the largest producer of imalees in the world.

J is for Jangal.

Rudyard Kipling wrote about the **jangal**, jungle, in his classic *The Jungle Book*, which was published in 1894. The book was inspired by his childhood years in India and is a collection of adventure stories involving animals.

K is for Kamal.

Kamal, lotus, is the national flower of India. Even though its roots and stem grow in mud, it holds its head, its flower, high and symbolizes wisdom and purity. It reminds us that even in hard times, our happiness and beauty remain within us.

L is for Ladakee.

Ladakees, girls, have pretty names. For example: Aditi, which means earth; Deepa, which means lamp; and Indu, which means moon.

M is for Machhalee.

India has over 4,500 miles of coastline and seven major rivers, and there are plenty of **machhalee**, fish, in the waters. Many people enjoy cooking and eating fish with Indian spices.

N is for Nirvaan.

Nirvaan is a state of being at peace in which you have no feelings or desires. It takes years of practice to still your mind so that you can reach this state.

O is for Om.

Om is a sacred sound or syllable that is repeated during prayers and meditations.

P is for Poppadoms.

Poppadoms are crispy lentil snacks that are served with chutneys or dipping sauces. These treats are the perfect accompaniment to any meal.

Q is for Qasam.

The prime minister of India takes a **qasam**,
an oath, before he or she begins the job:
". . . I will faithfully and conscientiously discharge
my duties as prime minister for the Union. . . ."

R is for Rupee.

The **rupee** is the currency of India, and its symbol is ₹. Mahatma Gandhi is India's founding father, and his image appears on currency circulating throughout the country.

S is for Sitar.

A **sitar** is an instrument made of wood and decorated with patterns. It can have more than twenty strings. Ravi Shankar was one of the most famous sitar players, and he performed with the Beatles. His daughter Anoushka Shankar is also a world famous sitarist.

T is for Tandoor.

A **tandoor** is a special oven made out of clay or metal that is used to cook breads or meats. The authors' favorite dish is tandoori chicken.

U is for Uttar Pradesh.

Uttar Pradesh is a state located in Northern India, and it has a population of almost two hundred million people. If it were a country, it would be the seventh largest in the world.

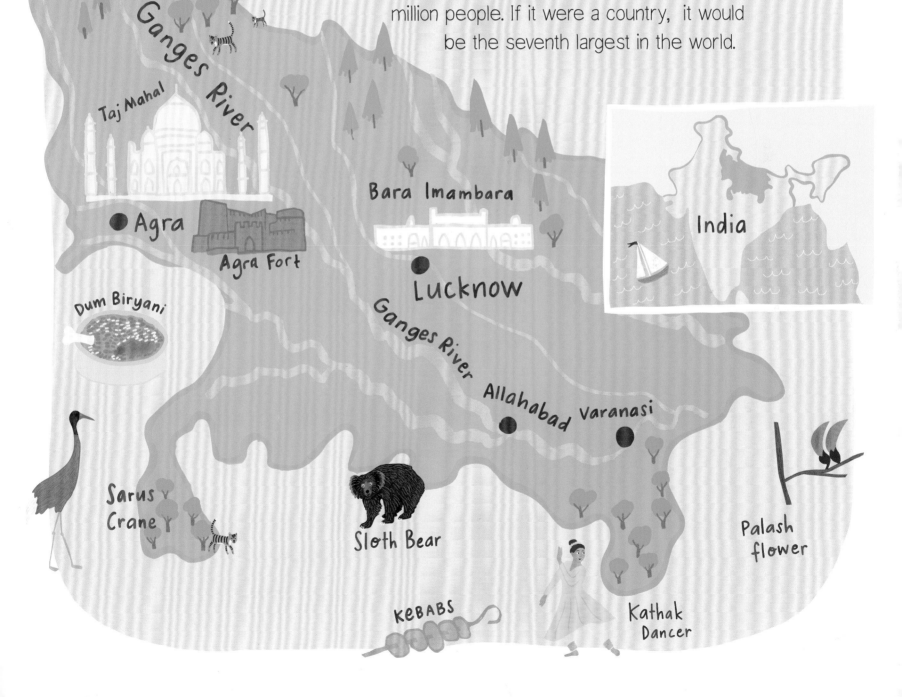

Ganges River

Taj Mahal

Agra

Agra Fort

Dum Biryani

Bara Imambara

Lucknow

India

Ganges River

Allahabad   Varanasi

Sarus Crane

Sloth Bear

KEBABS

Kathak Dancer

Palash flower

V is for Varanasi.

Varanasi is an ancient city in Uttar Pradesh, and it is located on the banks of the Ganges River. It's one of India's most sacred cities, and many go there on religious pilgrimages.

W is for Waraq.

Waraq is a silver or gold edible and flavorless foil that is a garnish on Indian sweets. It was originally used to prevent food from spoiling. It is also known as vark.

X is Laapata!

The letter X doesn't exist in Hindi like it does in English; it is **laapata**, missing, from the Hindi alphabet.

Y is for Yoga.

Yoga is a spiritual, mental, and physical practice in which you control your breath and do different poses with your body. Many practice yoga for health and relaxation.

Z is for Zaban.

Many different languages are spoken in India, including one called Urdu. "Zaban" is an Urdu word for language. With many different languages come many different ways of saying goodbye. Some of these include "alvida" (Urdu), "sat sri aakal" (Panjabi), "aawjo" (Gujarati), and "ta-ta" (British-Indian). The word "namaste" (Hindi) is also often used to say goodbye.

Sat sri aakal!

Alvida!

Aawjo!

Ta-ta!

Authors' Note

The two official languages of India are Hindi and English. Hindi is a melting-pot language that has absorbed words from other languages like Urdu, so some people refer to the language as "Hindustani." Hindi is the fourth largest natively spoken language in the world with 295 million speakers, after Mandarin, Spanish, and English. India has the second largest English speaking population in the world with 125 million, after the United States.

In fact, there are twenty-three languages used in India, and hundreds more when accounting for different dialects and various scripts. Hindi is written in the Devanagari alphabet, which is used for other languages too. For example, those from the state of Maharashtra speak Marathi, which is written using Devanagari. And those from Andhra Pradesh speak Telugu, which is written in Telugu script.

It's all very bhraamak (भ्रामक). That's Hindi for confusing.

It's also very uttejit karanevaala (उत्तेजित करनेवाला). That's Hindi for exciting!

Want to write the words in this book in Hindi? Here's how!

आम
Aam

बंदर
Bandar

चाय
Chai

दिवाली
Diwali

एक
Ek

फ़लूदा
Falooda

गुरु
Guru

हाथी
Haathee

इमली
Imalee

जंगल
Jangal

कमल
Kamal

लड़की
Ladakee

मछली
Machhalee

निर्वाण
Nirvaan

ओम
Om

पापड़
Poppadom

क़सम
Qasam

रुपया
Rupee

सितार
Sitar

तंदूर
Tandoor

उत्तर प्रदेश
Uttar Pradesh

वाराणसी
Varanasi

वरक़
Waraq

लापता
Laapata

योग
Yoga

ज़बान
Zaban

To Nora and Finn,
who spellbind us with their creativity
—S. S. & K. S.

For my Dad,
who always enjoyed a good poppadom
—H. I.

BEACH LANE BOOKS
An imprint of Simon & Schuster Children's Publishing Division
1230 Avenue of the Americas, New York, New York 10020
Text copyright © 2019 by Kabir Sehgal and Surishtha Sehgal
Illustrations copyright © 2019 by Hazel Ito
BEACH LANE BOOKS is a trademark of Simon & Schuster, Inc.
For information about special discounts for bulk purchases, please contact Simon & Schuster Special Sales
at 1-866-506-1949 or business@simonandschuster.com.
The Simon & Schuster Speakers Bureau can bring authors to your live event.
For more information or to book an event, contact the Simon & Schuster Speakers Bureau
at 1-866-248-3049 or visit our website at www.simonspeakers.com.
Book design by Lauren Rille
The text for this book was set in Write and Bizzle Chizzle.
The illustrations for this book were rendered digitally.
Manufactured in China
0819 SCP
First Edition
2 4 6 8 10 9 7 5 3 1
Library of Congress Cataloging-in-Publication Data
Names: Sehgal, Kabir, author. | Sehgal, Surishtha, author. | Ito, Hazel, illustrator.
Title: P is for poppadoms : an Indian alphabet book / Kabir Sehgal and Surishtha Sehgal ; illustrated by Hazel Ito.
Other titles: P is for pappadams | P is for papadums | Indian alphabet book
Description: New York : Beach Lane Books, [2019] | Includes bibliographical references and index. |
Audience: Grades K–3. | Audience: Ages 0–8.
Identifiers: LCCN 2019000749 | ISBN 9781534421721 (hardcover : alk. paper) | ISBN 9781534421738 (eBook)
Subjects: LCSH: India—Civilization—Juvenile literature. | Alphabet books—India—Juvenile literature. |
India—Juvenile poetry. | English language—Alphabet—Juvenile literature.
Classification: LCC DS423.S3325 2019 | DDC 954—dc23
LC record available at https://lccn.loc.gov/2019000749